Run, Rabbit, Run!

Turn the page to start the story.

I spot six crocs
in the park today.

"Hey! Play on the train with us," they say.

I see seven vultures
high in the sky.

"Ooh, can you fly?
We will help you try!"

"Jump in our boat,
we will go for a row."

"Slow, so slow,
just dip in your toe..."

19

Three sharks swim
in the new blue pool.

21

"The sun is hot, but you can keep cool."

"Shoo!" I say.
"I am not such a fool."

Puzzle 1

Look at the pictures, then choose
the right sentence for each one.

1.

A "Crayon the train with us."

B "Play on the train with us."

2.

A "Join us for a feast."

B "Join us for a beast."

3.

A "Ooh, can you fly?"

B "Ooh, can you fry?"

4.

A "You can keep cool."

B "You can keep wool."

Puzzle 2

Choose the right speech bubbles for the little animals to warn Rabbit.

1.

2.

3.

Puzzle 3

There is one word in each group that **doesn't** rhyme with the rest. Can you spot it?

1. | hey | fly | play | say |

2. | see | me | tie | tree |

3. | sky | say | high | lie |

4. | too | go | slow | toe |

5. | you | new | row | blue |

Answers to puzzles

Puzzle 1

1. B "Play on the train with us."
2. A "Join us for a feast."
3. A "Ooh, can you fly?"
4. A "You can keep cool."

Puzzle 2

1. "Stay away!"
2. "Better not wait and see!"
3. "That's a lie!"
4. "No! No! No!"

Puzzle 3

1. fly
2. tie
3. say
4. too
5. row

Guidance notes

Usborne Very First Reading is a series of books, specially developed for children who are learning to read. **Run, Rabbit, Run!** is the ninth book in the series, and by this stage your child should be able to read the story alone, with occasional help from you.

The story of **Run, Rabbit, Run!** introduces different spellings of the five sounds shown below:

Later books in the series gradually introduce more ways of spelling these and other sounds, while reinforcing the ones your child already knows.

You'll find lots more information about the structure of the series, advice on helping your child with reading, extra practice activities and games on the Very First Reading website,* **www.usborne.com/veryfirstreading**

*US readers go to **www.veryfirstreading.com**

Some questions and answers

- **Why do I need to read with my child?**
  Sharing stories makes reading an enjoyable
  and fun activity for children. It also helps them
  to develop confidence and stamina. Even if you
  are not taking an active part in reading, your
  listening and support are very important.

- **When is a good time to read?**
  Choose a time when you are both relaxed, but
  not too tired, and there are no distractions.
  Only read for as long as your child wants to –
  you can always try again another day.

- **What if my child gets stuck?**
  Don't simply read the problem word yourself,
  but prompt your child and try to find the right
  answer together. Similarly, if your child makes
  a mistake, go back and look at the word
  together. Don't forget to give plenty of praise
  and encouragement.

- **We've finished, now what do we do?**
  It's a good idea to read the story several times
  to give your child more practice and more
  confidence. Then, when your child is ready,
  you can go on to the next book in the series,
  Late Night at the Zoo.

Edited by Jenny Tyler and Lesley Sims
Designed by Caroline Spatz

This edition first published in 2013 by Usborne Publishing Ltd.,
Usborne House, 83-85 Saffron Hill, London EC1N 8RT, England.
www.usborne.com Copyright © 2013, 2010 Usborne Publishing Ltd.

32